BUDDHA AND THE ROSE

Written by
MALLIKA CHOPRA

Illustrated by
NEHA RAWAT

RP|KIDS
PHILADELPHIA

To my sweet babies, now young ladies. I love you,
Tara and Leela.
—M. C.

For Ma & Pa, thank you for always supporting me and
being my biggest cheerleaders.
—N. R.

Running Press Kids
Hachette Book Group
1290 Avenue of the Americas, New York, NY 10104
www.runningpress.com/rpkids
@RP_Kids

Printed in China

First Edition: September 2022

Published by Running Press Kids, an imprint of Perseus Books, LLC, a subsidiary of Hachette Book Group, Inc.
The Running Press Kids name and logo is a trademark of the Hachette Book Group.

The Hachette Speakers Bureau provides a wide range of authors for speaking events.
To find out more, go to www.hachettespeakersbureau.com or call (866) 376-6591.

The publisher is not responsible for websites (or their content) that are not owned by the publisher.

Print book cover and interior design by Frances J. Soo Ping Chow.

Library of Congress Cataloging-in-Publication Data
Names: Chopra, Mallika, author. | Rawat, Neha, illustrator. Title: Buddha and the rose / written by Mallika Chopra;
illustrated by Neha Rawat. Description: First edition. | Philadelphia : Running Press Kids, 2022. | Audience: Ages 4-8. |
Summary: Sujata, a milkmaid, observes the Buddha smiling at a single rose, and, closing her eyes, begins to truly perceive the world
around her, and her connection to all of the universe. Identifiers: LCCN 2021033883 (print) | LCCN 2021033884 (ebook) |
ISBN 9780762478767 (hardcover) | ISBN 9780762478774 (ebook) | ISBN 9780762478811 (ebook) | ISBN 9780762478828 (ebook)
Subjects: LCSH: Gautama Buddha—Juvenile fiction. | Buddhism—Juvenile fiction. | Spiritual life—Buddhism—Juvenile fiction. | CYAC:
Buddha—Fiction. | Buddhism—Fiction. | Spiritual life—Fiction. Classification: LCC PZ7.1.C5423 Bu 2022 (print) | LCC PZ7.1.C5423 (ebook) |
DDC [E]—dc23 LC record available at https://lccn.loc.gov/2021033883 LC ebook record available at https://lccn.loc.gov/2021033884

ISBNs: 978-0-7624-7876-7 (hardcover), 978-0-7624-7877-4 (ebook),
978-0-7624-7881-1 (ebook), 978-0-7624-7882-8 (ebook)

1010

10 9 8 7 6 5 4 3 2 1

AUTHOR'S NOTE

Buddha was a teacher who lived more than 2,500 years ago. He helped people see the world differently, with more love and compassion. People came to visit him from distant lands to hear his words, to be inspired, to find comfort in their suffering, and to understand their purpose in life.

This story of *Buddha and the Rose* is adapted from one of his famous talks. It is told from the perspective of Sujata, a milkmaid who brought Buddha the rice pudding to break his fast after meditating on the nature of existence. Sujata could be considered Buddha's first student.

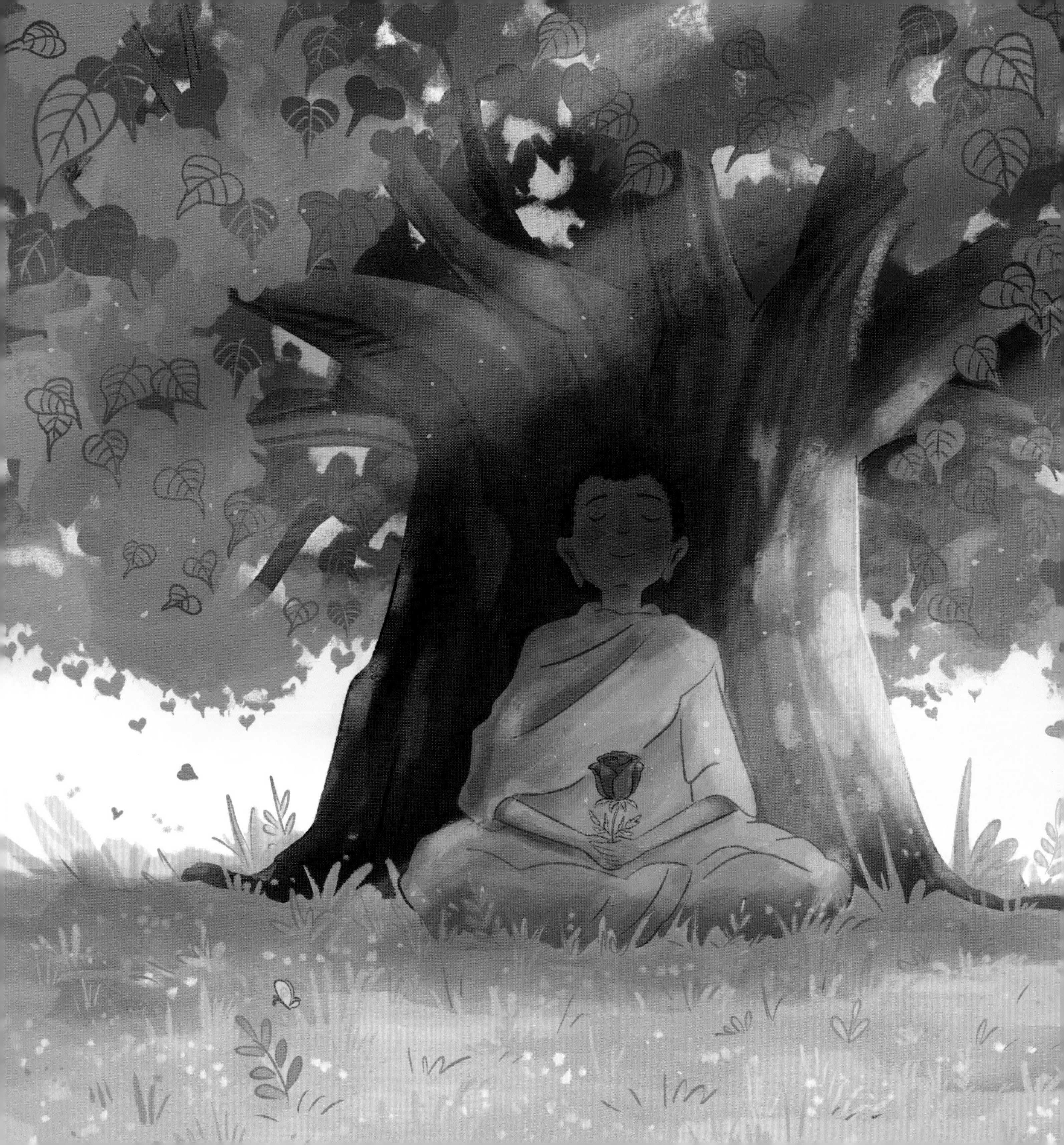

Buddha sat.
A rose in his hand. Still.

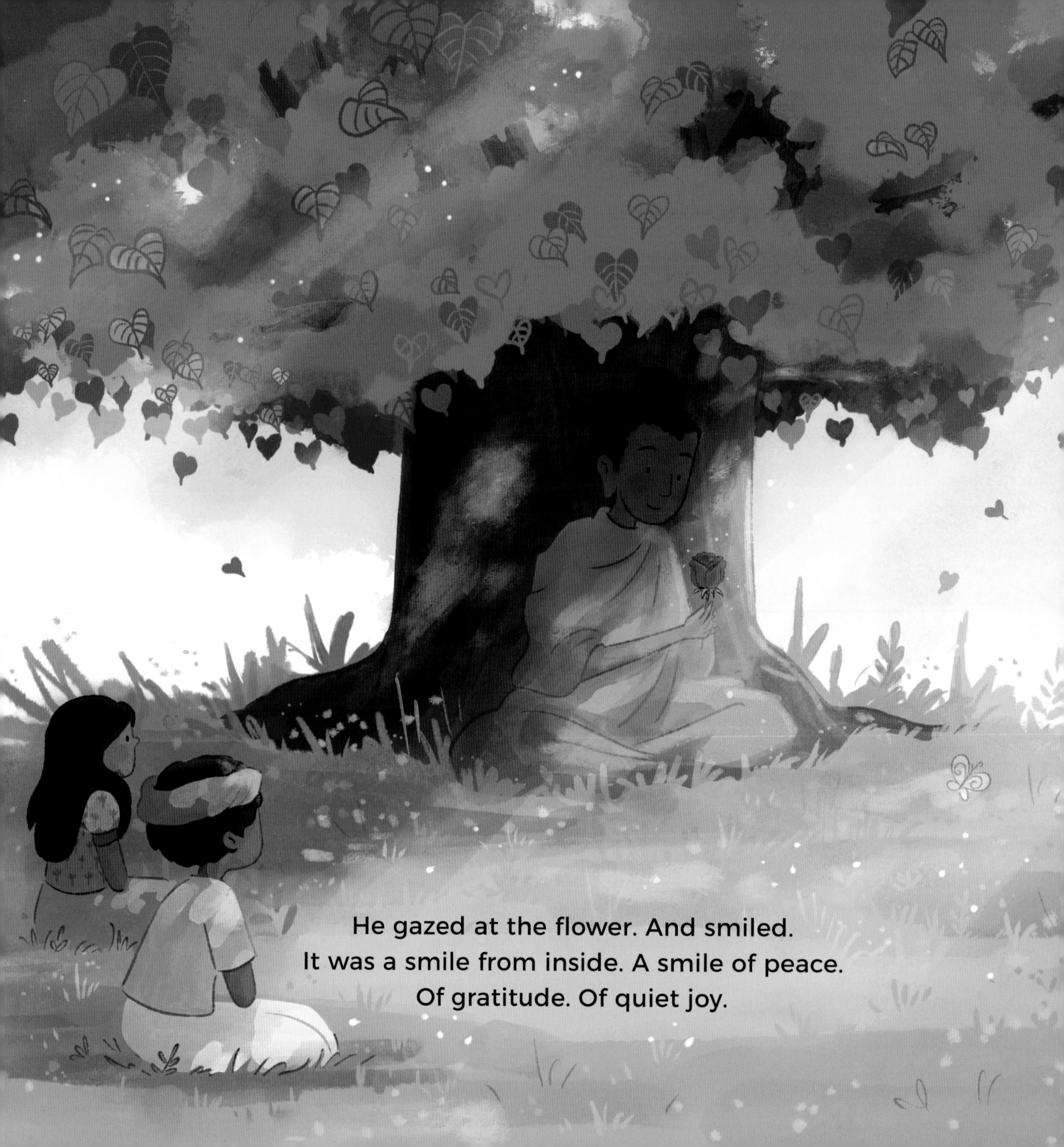

He gazed at the flower. And smiled.
It was a smile from inside. A smile of peace.
Of gratitude. Of quiet joy.

A smile that swept across the crowd.
And the feeling was happiness.

He turned to all of us. And waited.
Patiently. For us to see.

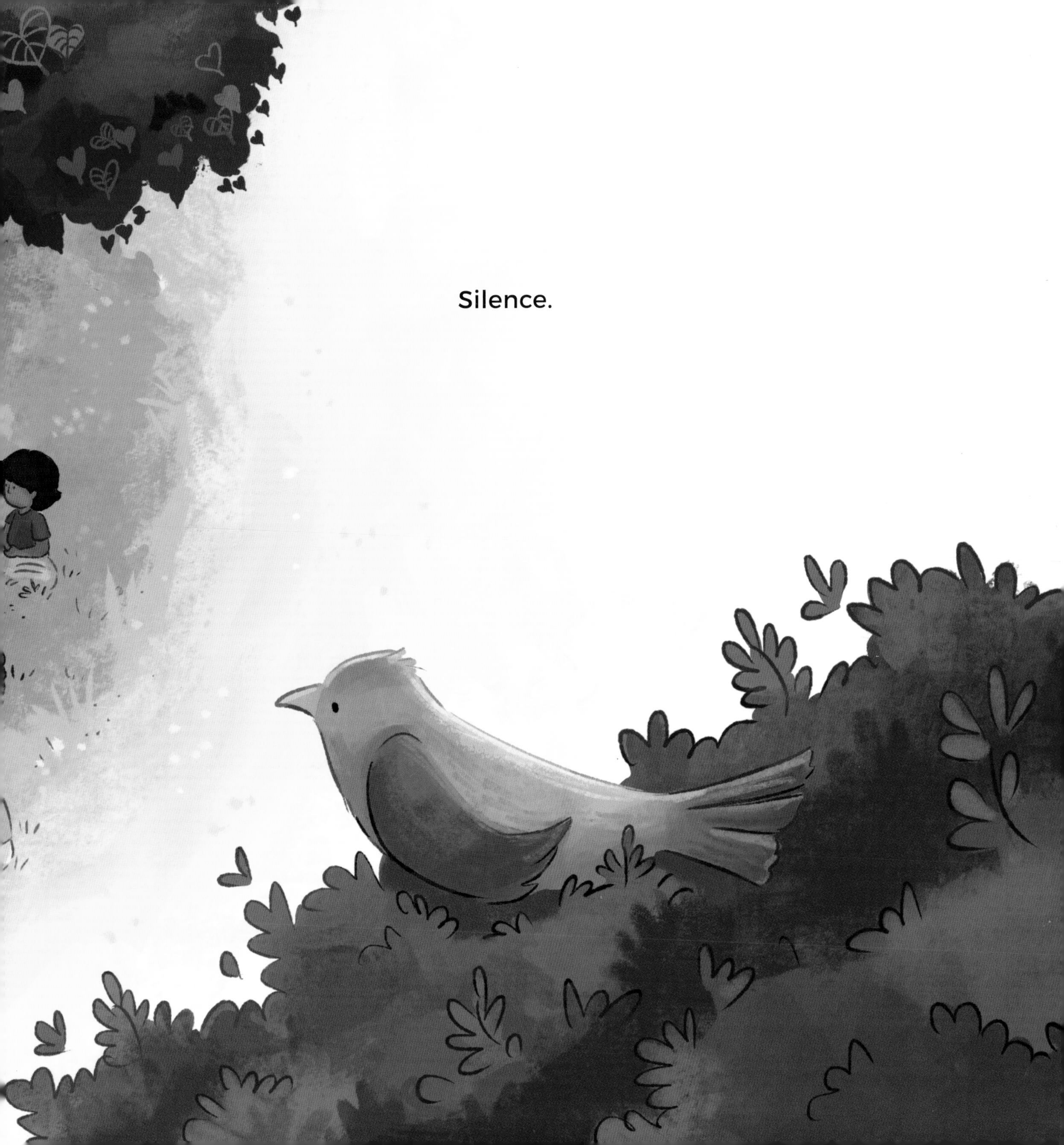

Silence.

I could hear the wind, the breathing of those around me.
Someone said, "I don't understand.
What does he mean?"

Another whispered, "Why isn't he saying anything?"

He sat. Still silent.
No words. Present. Just being.

I looked at the rose in his hand.
I was confused, so I closed my eyes. I took a breath.
In . . . and . . . out. I opened my eyes.

And I saw it!
In that moment I felt totally awake, alive,
like I had never felt before.

And I saw the rose in all its glory.

I saw the deep, rich colors of each rose petal.
The petals perfectly placed, giving the flower its special shape.

I smelled the scent of the rose drifting toward me.
A perfume sweet, delicate, yet so powerful.

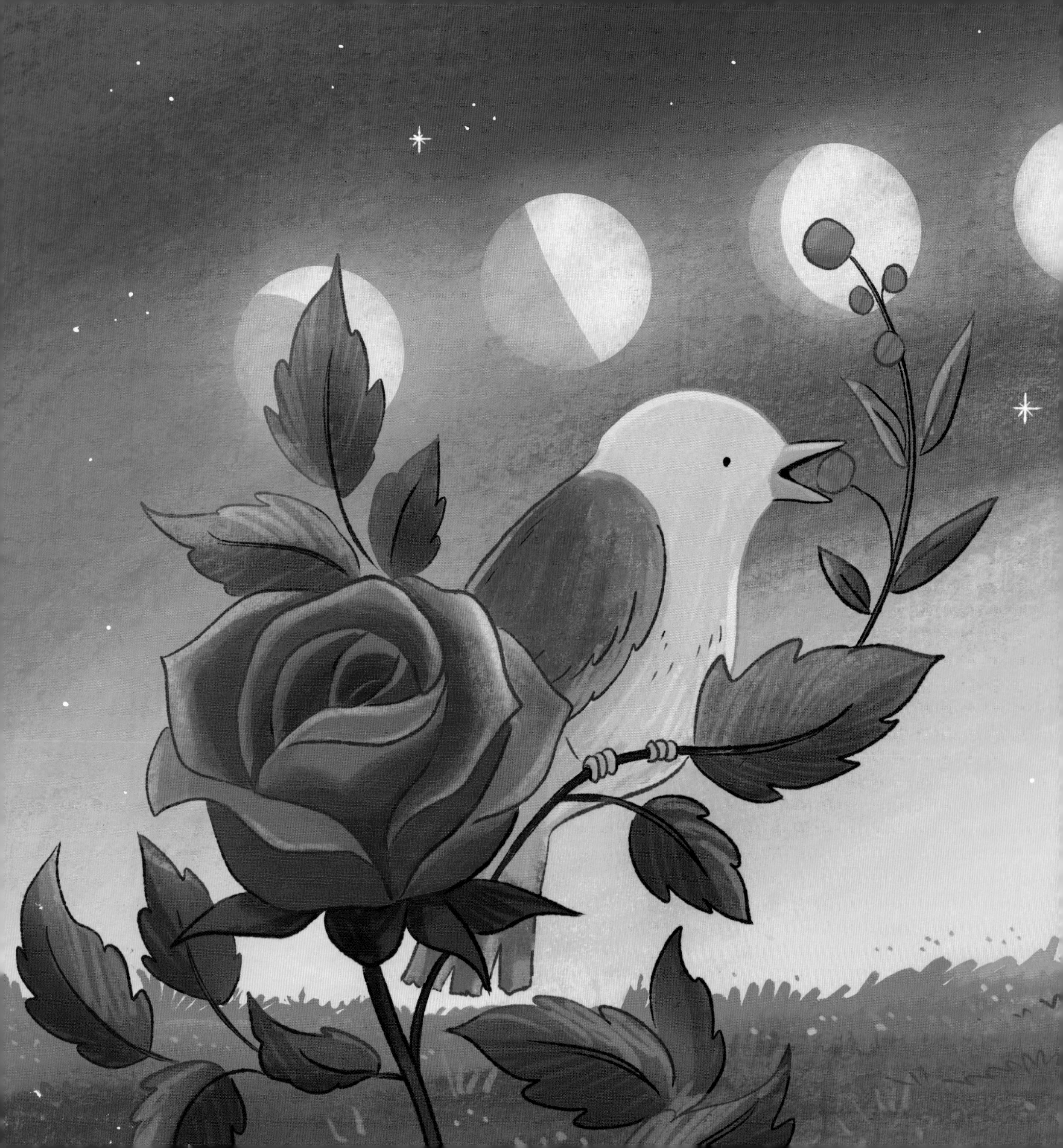

And I sensed its journey.
A seed that had traveled through space and time
to find its sacred place in the ground.

I felt the warmth of the sun on the dirt.
The energy flowing up through its stem, its thorns, and its leaves.

I felt the coolness of the black night, glittering with all the stars in the galaxy. I felt the moment before the seed chose to blossom into a flower.

I saw the clouds, the rain, and the rainbows.
I saw a double rainbow.

I saw the insects feeding the soil.
I heard birds singing and dancing in circles around the rose.

And there were the bees,
making sweet honey.

I saw children sweetening their food
with the same honey.

I saw beautiful flowers in the temple and at festivals.
People praying, dancing, and celebrating.

I saw couples marrying, with garlands on their necks
and rose petals spread on the ground by their feet.
I felt love. Joy. Eternity.

Ah! I closed my eyes.
Taking in a beauty I never before knew existed.

As I opened my eyes, I gasped! I saw.
I saw *myself* looking at the rose.

I saw the Earth, the sun, the stars, and the galaxy around me. .
And I knew I was magic and special—just like the rose.

I felt grateful for all that had brought me to this place, to this moment, to truly *see* the rose. To truly *see* myself as a part of the whole of this magnificent universe.

I looked at Buddha's face and saw that he knew I understood.
And all I could do was smile.

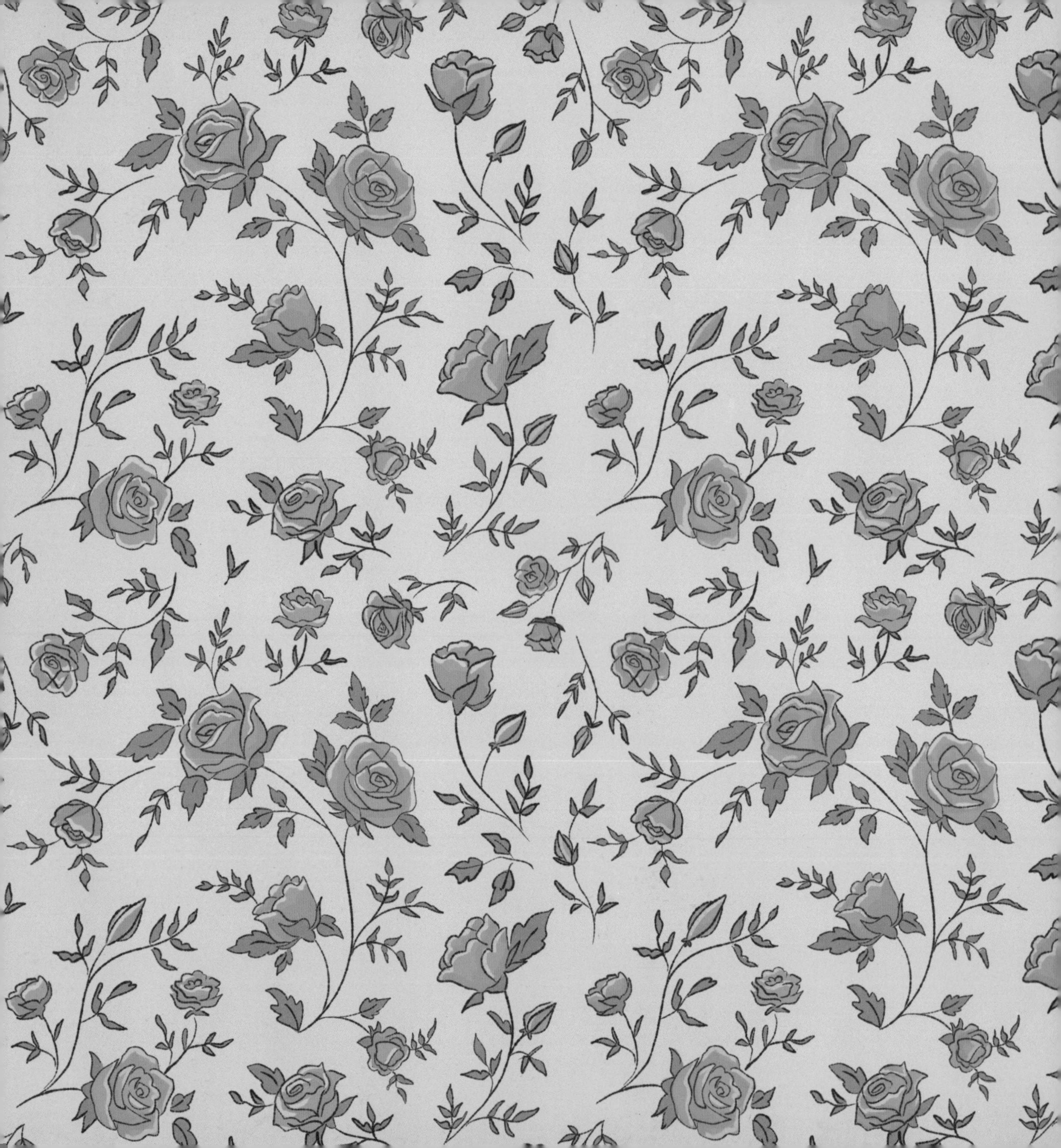